by

Sherrill S. Cannon

Illustrations by Kalpart

Strategic Book Publishing and Rights Co.

Copyright © 2013
All rights reserved by Sherrill S. Cannon.

Book Design/Layout, Illustrations and Book Cover design by Kalpart.
Visit www.kalpart.com

No part of this book may be reproduced or transmitted in any form or by any means, graphic, electronic, or mechanical, including photocopying, recording, taping, or by any information storage retrieval system, without the permission, in writing, from the publisher.

Strategic Book Publishing and Rights Co.
12620 FM 1960, Suite A4-507
Houston, TX 77065
www.sbpra.com

ISBN: 978-1-62212-478-7

For
Cristiano Cannon
who asked me to write
a story about a
superhero!

And also for my other grands:
Chloe Grey
Kylie Brenna, Mikaila Bryn, Kelsey Beth,
Tucker Flynn, Lindsay Alexis
Colby Stalker, Parker James, Joshua Cakebread

I was unhappy, for Rob took my toy,

Just grabbed it away with a look full of joy.

So I told my mother who said, "That's not nice,"

And then tried to give me some helpful advice.

She told me that I should stand up for what's right,

And to think about that while in bed for the night.

So when I lay down in my soft little bed,

I tried hard to think about what Mom had said.

I closed my eyes tight and I promised myself

To stand for what's right and to give others help,

And thought I heard something as I fell asleep,

A voice in my head that seemed to repeat . . .

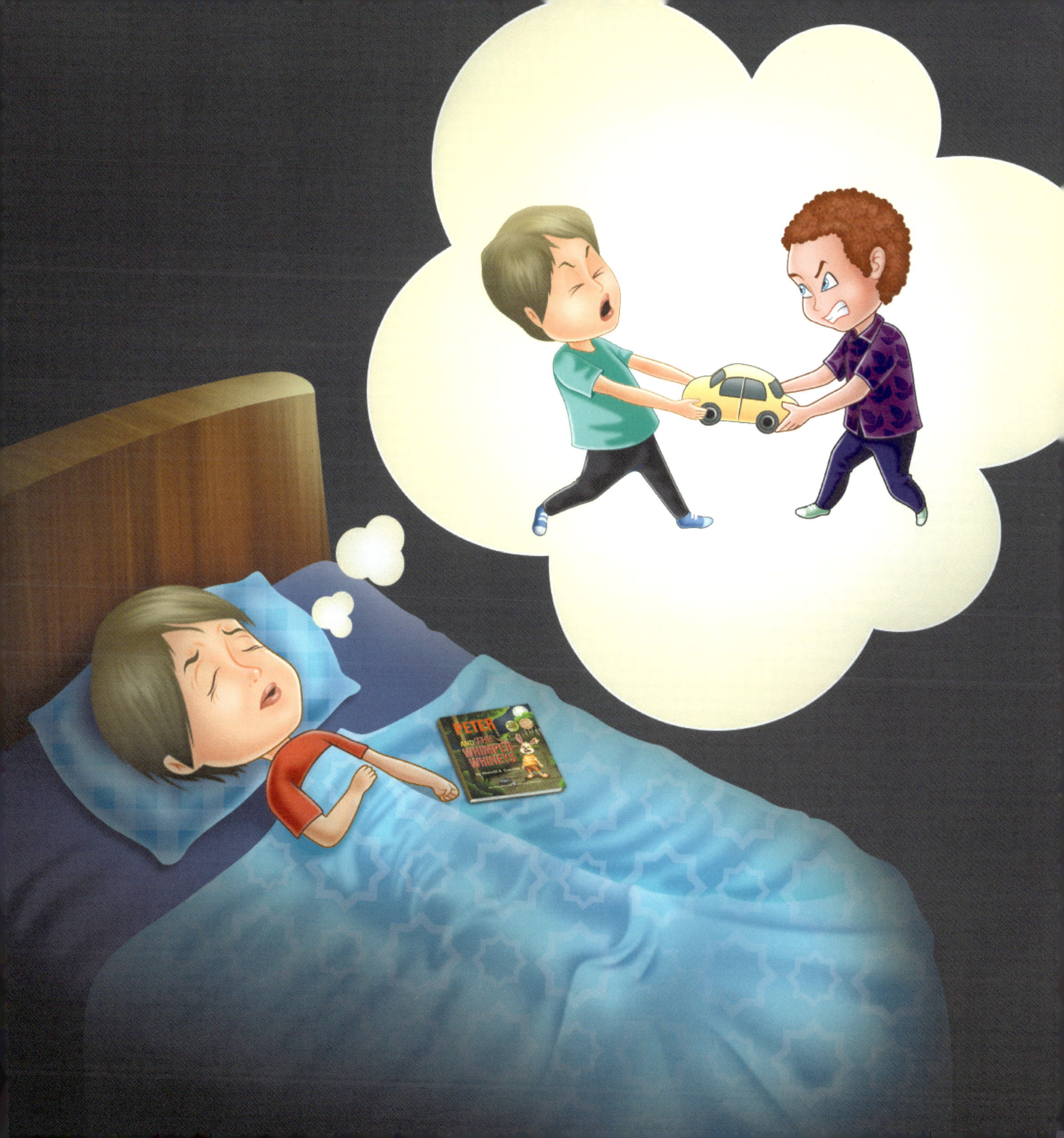
PETER
AND THE
WHIMPER-
WHINEYS

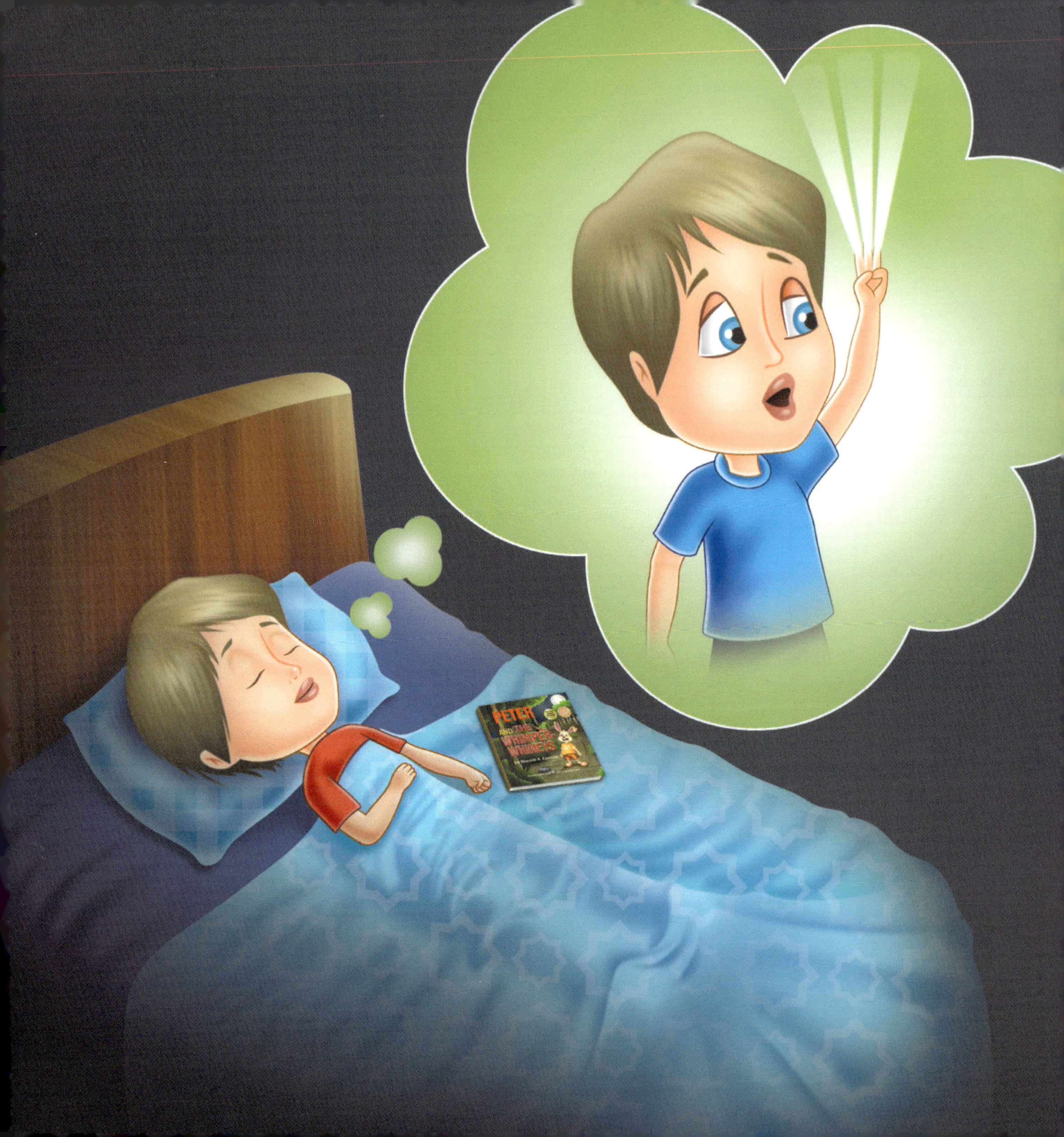
PETER
AND THE
WHIMPER-
WHINEYS

"Call upon Manner-Man; he'll save the day
And help all good children to share when they play.
This hero's within you; when you raise your hand,
Your fingertips' flash will help them understand
That thinking of others and being polite
And doing for others what you know you'd like,
Will help you be happy and make many friends
And feel so much better when bullying ends.
Just say, 'I am strong, and my flash is bright,
And I will defend you and make things all right.'"

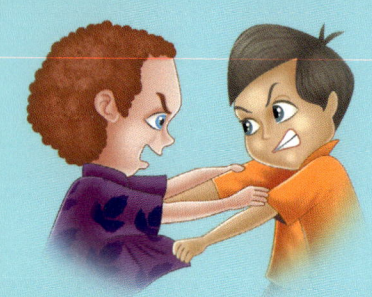

Imagine my wonder the very next day
When I went to my school and then went out to play,
I found that my dream seemed to really come true;
When I saw children fighting, I knew what to do.
I said, "I am strong, and my flash is bright,
And I will defend you and make things all right."
I put up my hand, from the tips came a flash,
And Manner-Man came, just as if I had asked.
He stopped all the fighting and arguing too,
And then he told them what they needed to do:

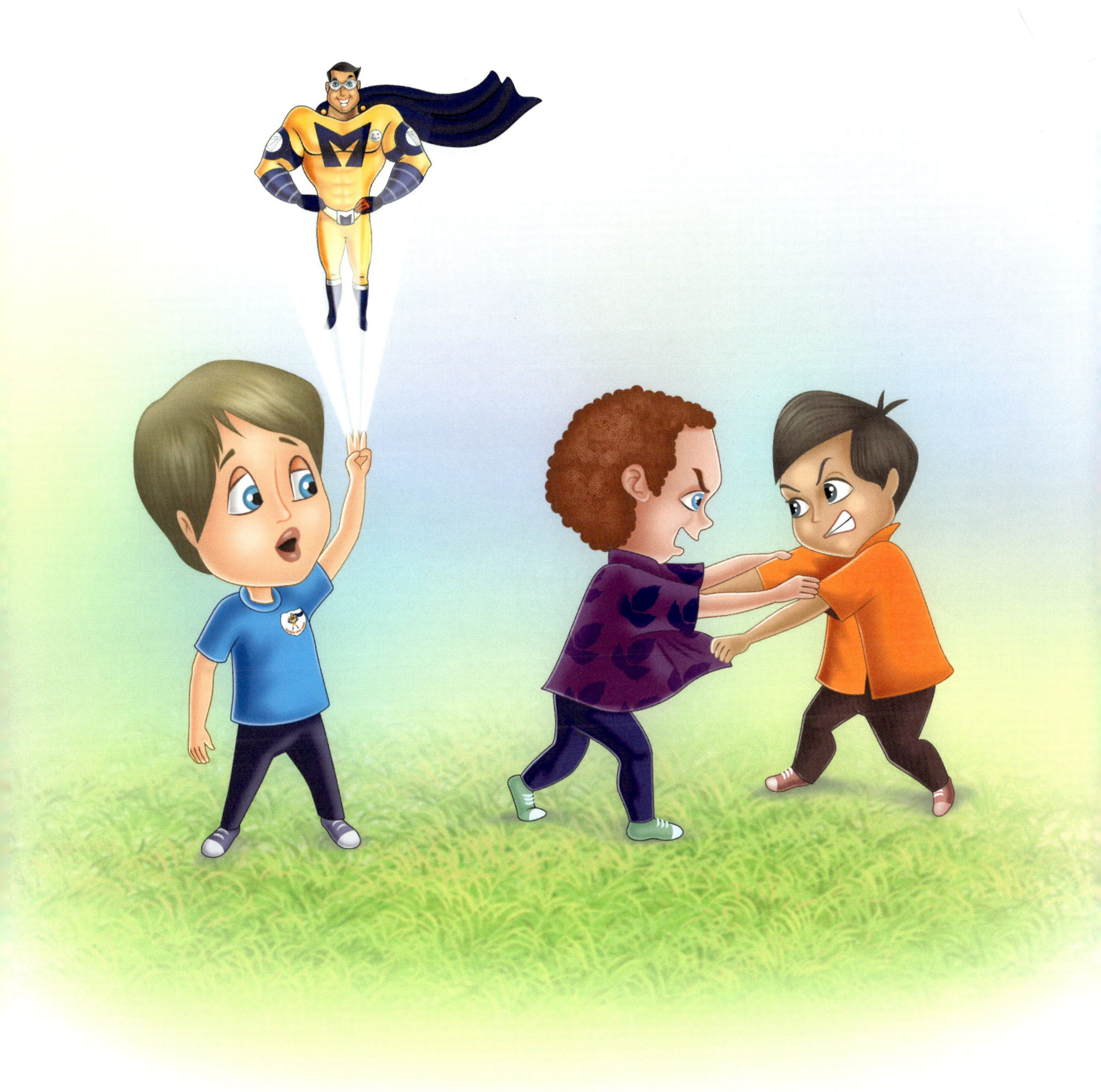

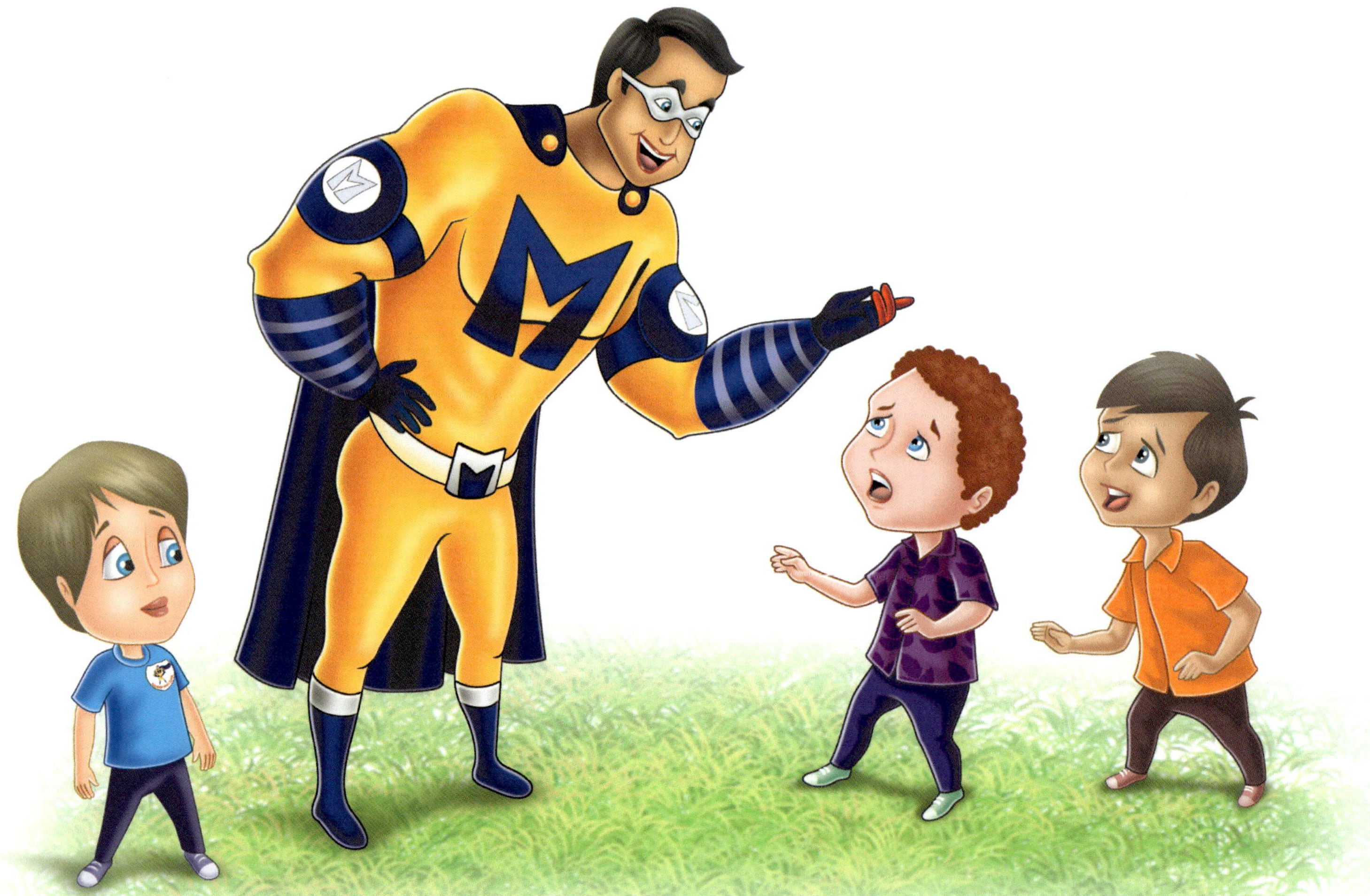

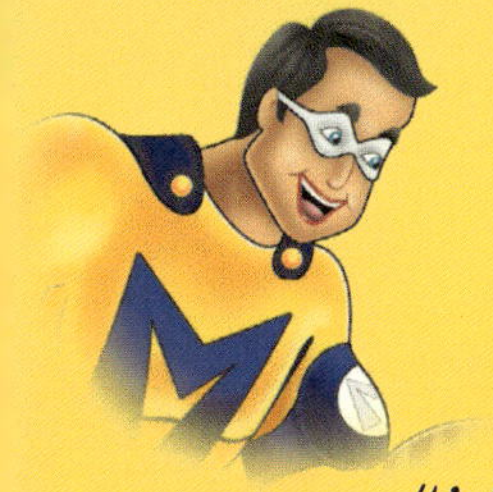

"When facing a problem," he said, "use your words,
Instead of just punching when fighting occurs.
If somebody pushes you, don't you push back.
Just say, 'Not nice' to stop an attack.
Try hard to share, but if someone just takes,
Ask Manner-Man to correct those mistakes.
Tell your friend, 'Wait, please, until I am done;
Then I will share, and we'll both have more fun.'"
Manner-Man then said, "You must take your turn.
Don't butt into lines, but just try hard to learn
That sharing is more fun, and caring is cool . . .
And soon you will find you have more fun at school!"

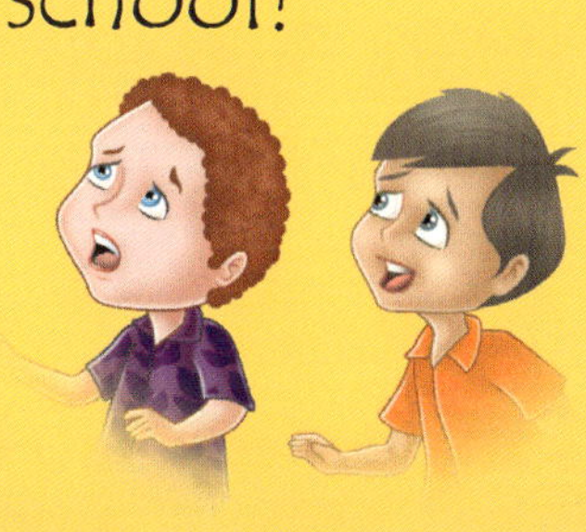

My new hero Manner-Man's big and he's strong.
He helps to teach children what's right and what's wrong.
He teaches good manners, so take his advice:
If someone starts hitting, just shout out, "Not nice!"

But also be careful to not hit with words,
For sometimes that hurts worse each time it occurs.
To call people names that are not very kind,
Will hurt your friends' feelings, I think you will find.

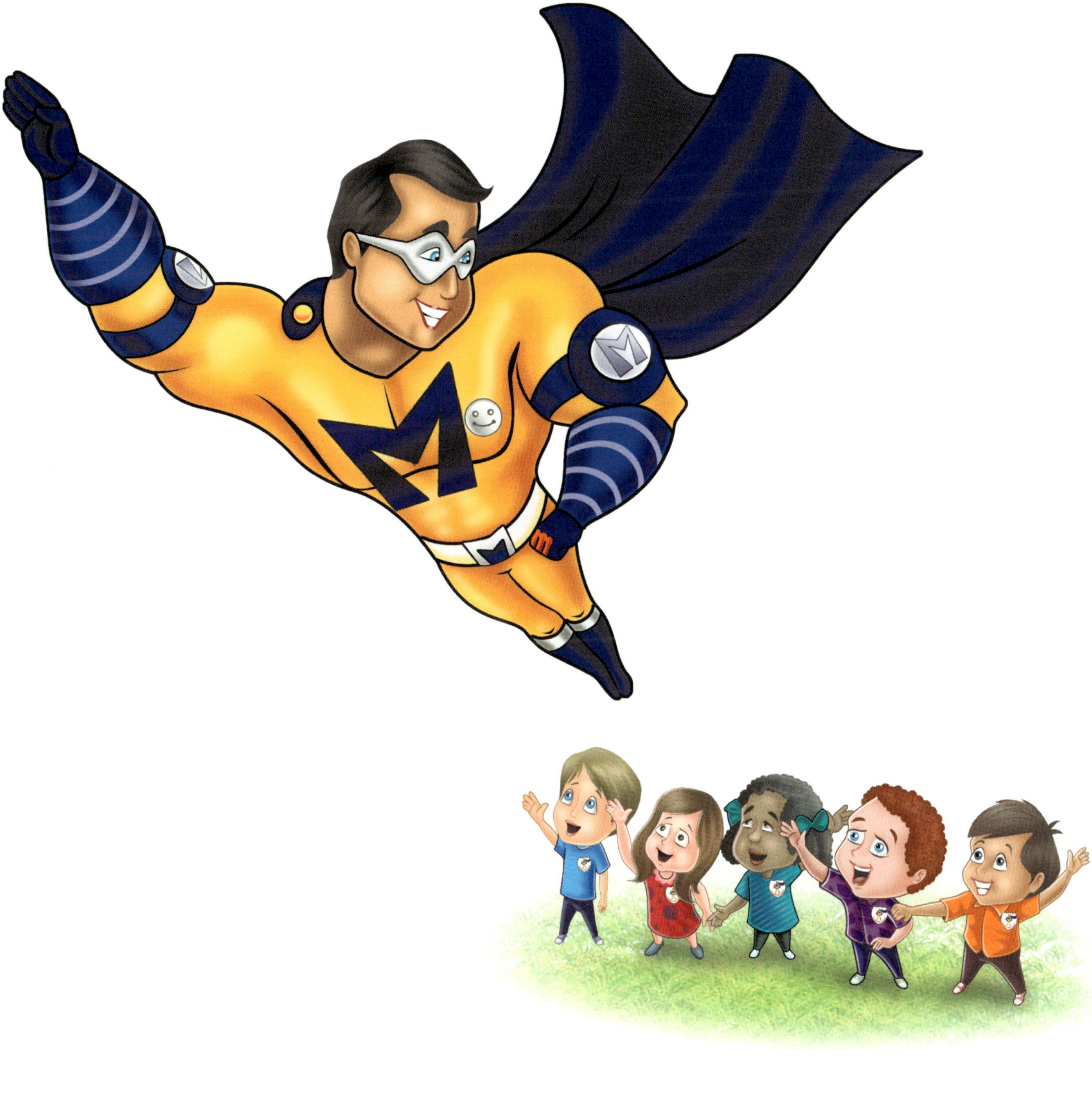

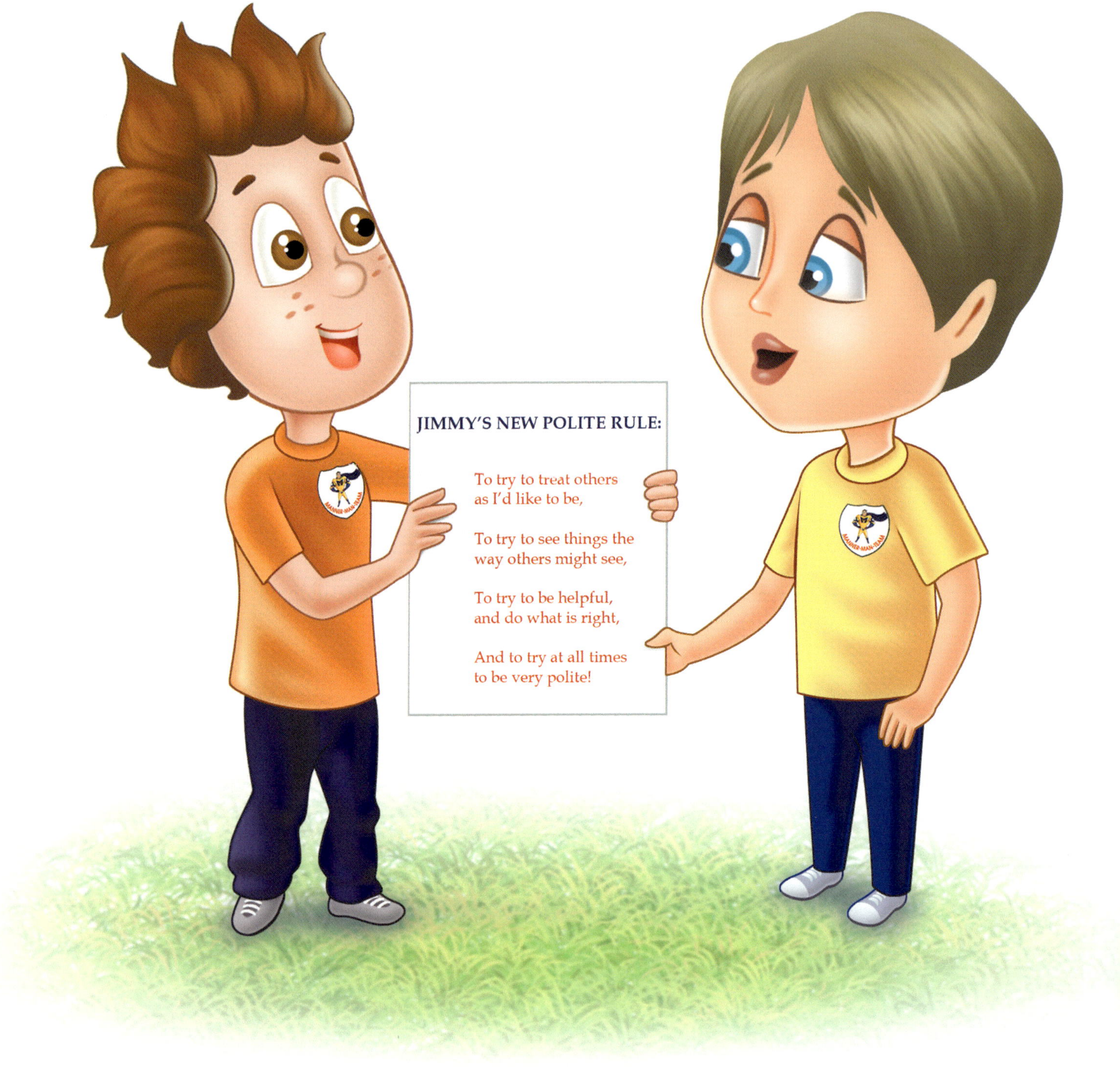
JIMMY'S NEW POLITE RULE:
To try to treat others
as I'd like to be,
To try to see things the
way others might see,
To try to be helpful,
and do what is right,
And to try at all times
to be very polite!

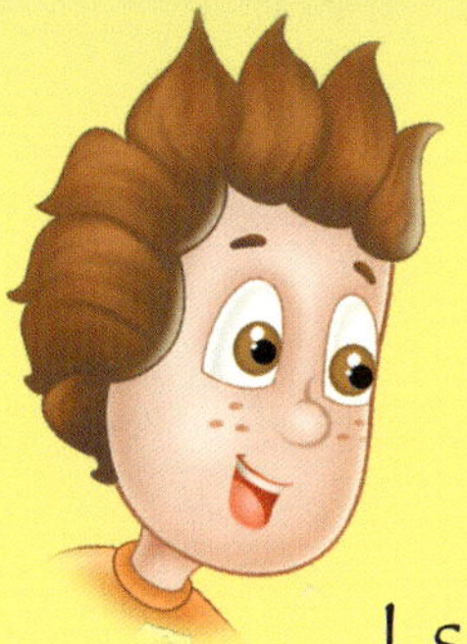

I saw my friend Jimmy, who now is called James;
He's happy because now he joins in the games.
He once was a bully who grabbed and said "Gimme,"
But now is polite and no longer called Jimmy.
James said he'd like to use Manner-Man too,
To help to teach others his "New Polite Rule."
I told him my secret, helped him learn the way
To call upon Manner-Man, help save the day,
Just say, "I am strong, and my flash is bright,
And I will defend you and make things all right."
So James is now part of my Manner-Man Team,
Rescuing kids from the ones who are mean.

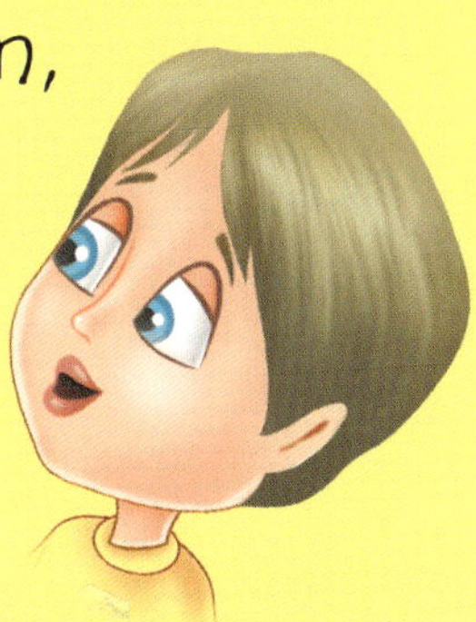

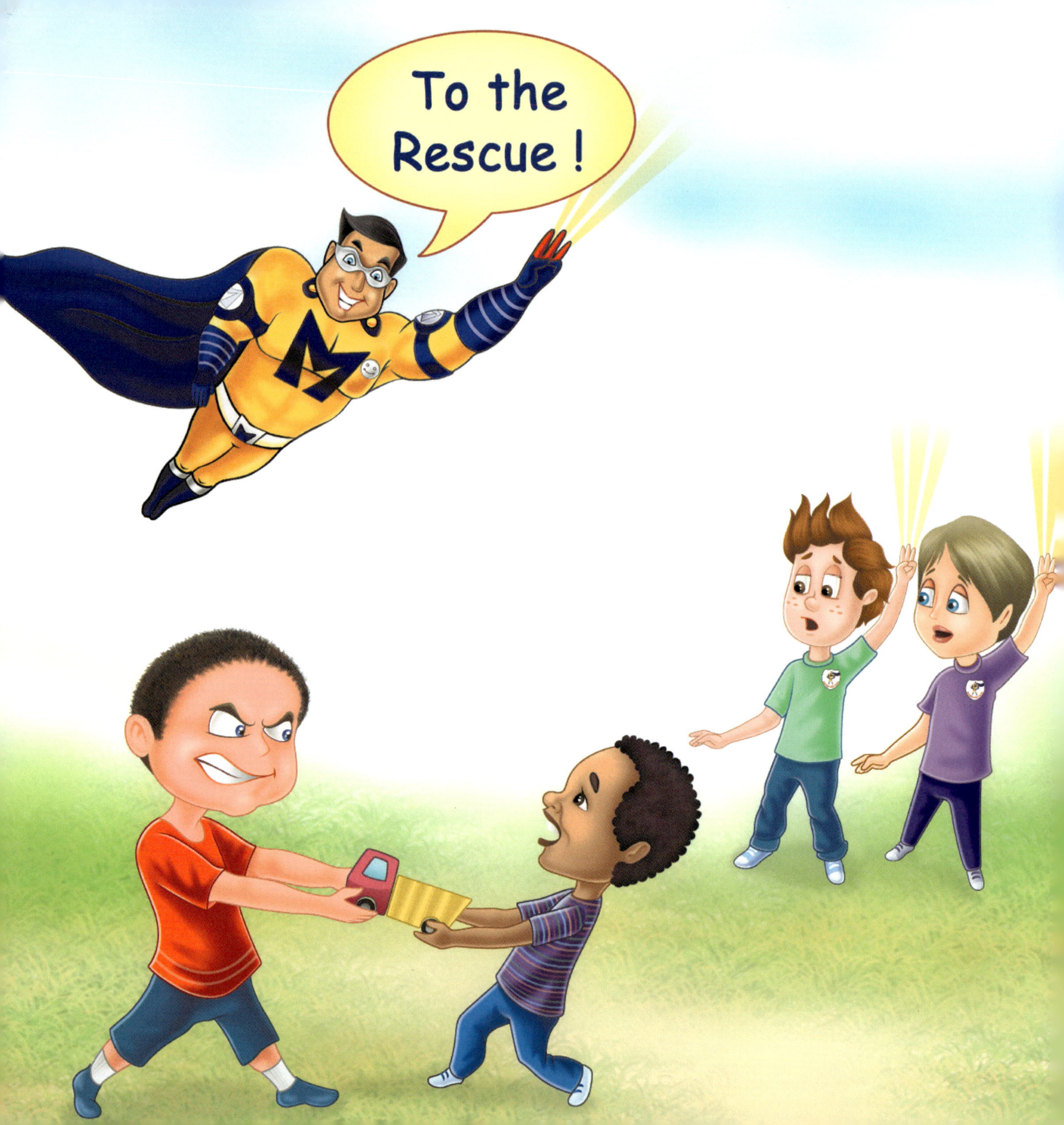
To the Rescue !

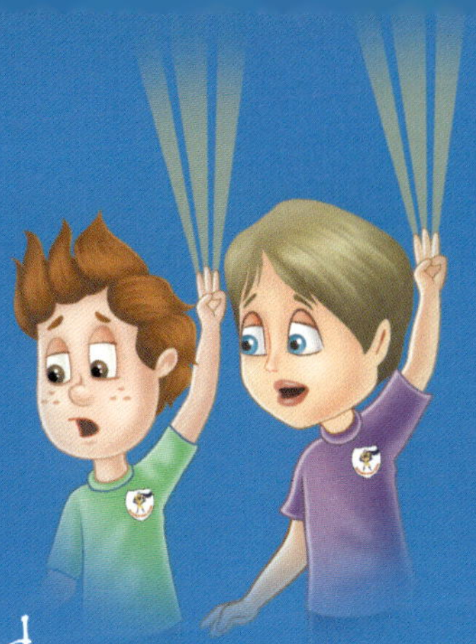

Our new superhero is now our best friend.
He looks for the bad guys, and he helps us win.
He teaches good manners, so take his advice:
If someone starts pushing, just shout out, "Not nice!"

For sometimes a bully will grab all the toys,
Not leaving any for good girls and boys.
Just call for Manner-Man, he will help you;
Manner-Man comes, calling "To the rescue!"

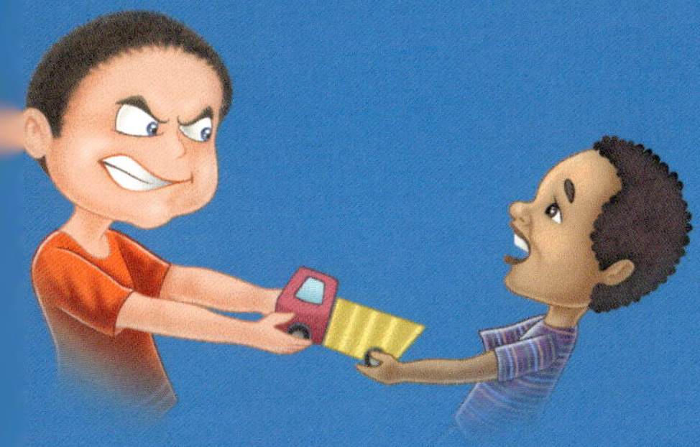

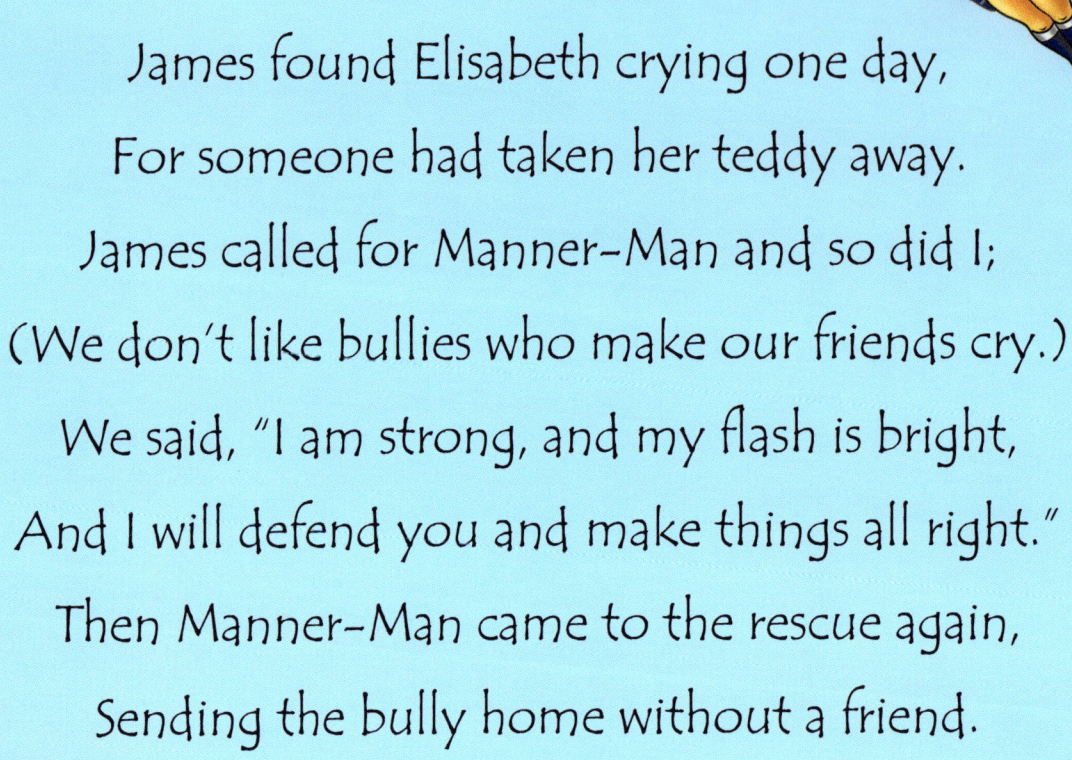

James found Elisabeth crying one day,
For someone had taken her teddy away.
James called for Manner-Man and so did I;
(We don't like bullies who make our friends cry.)
We said, "I am strong, and my flash is bright,
And I will defend you and make things all right."
Then Manner-Man came to the rescue again,
Sending the bully home without a friend.

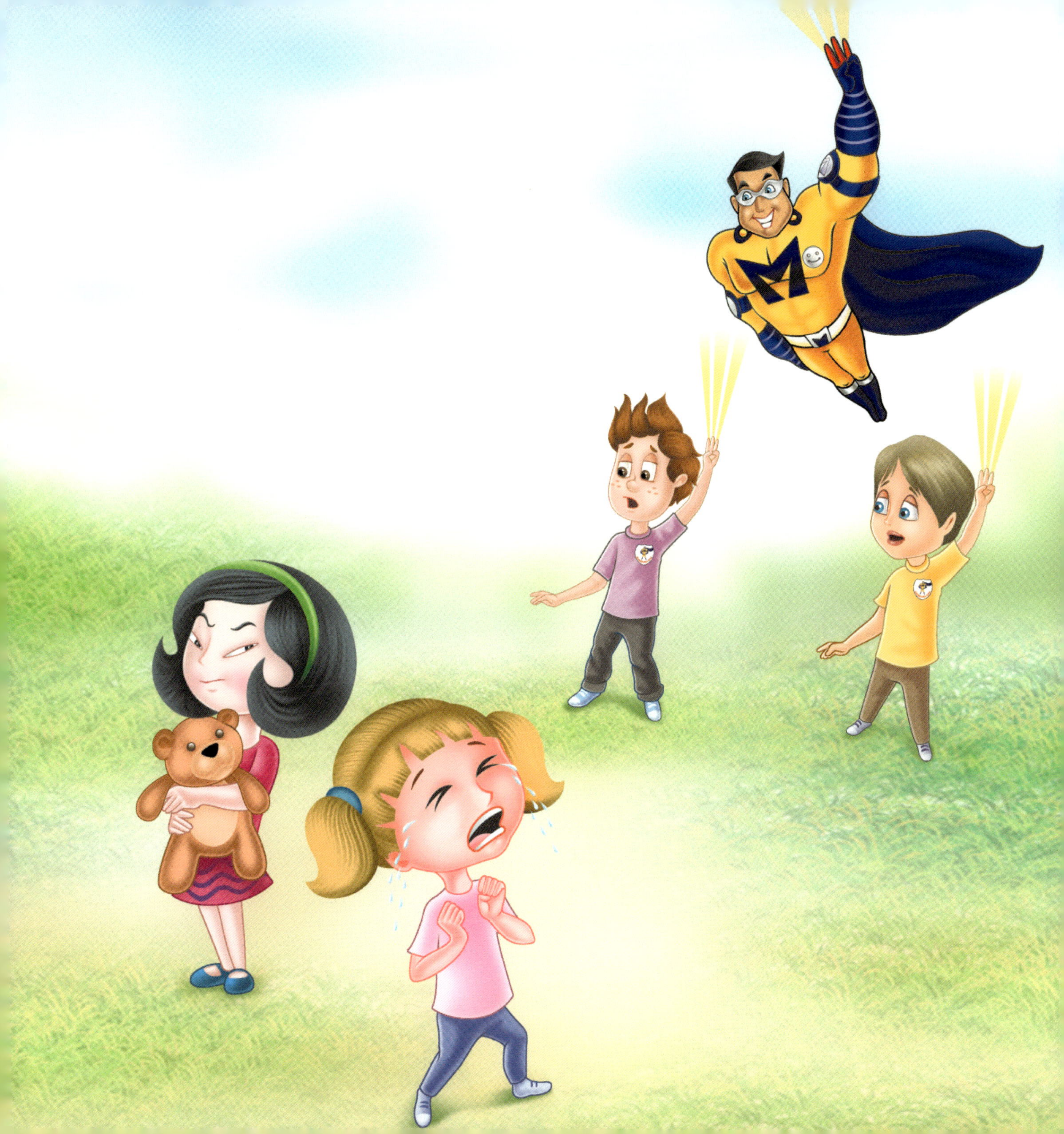

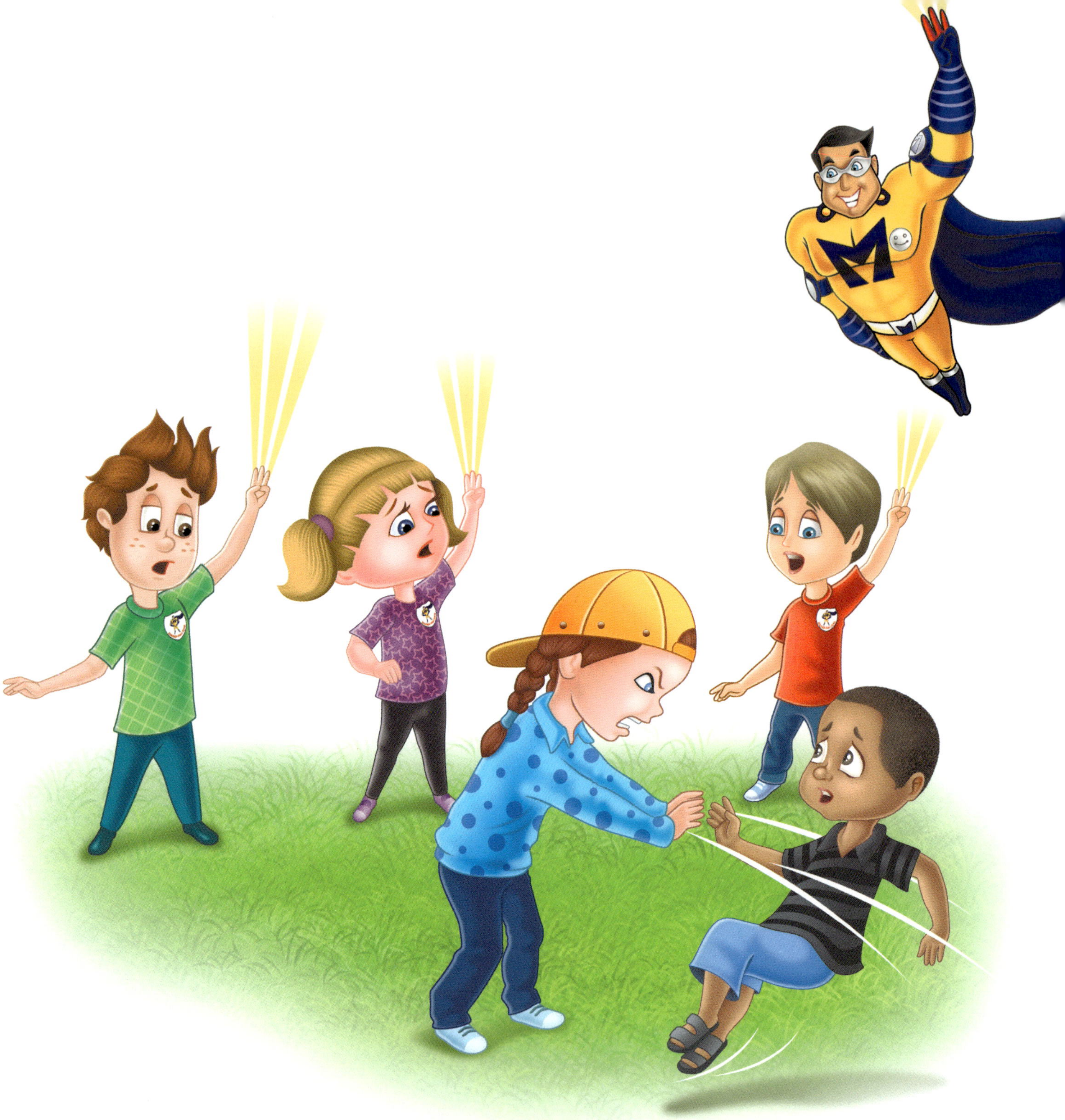

Elisabeth asked to use Manner-Man too
To help teach her friends to say "please" and "thank you."
We told her our secret, helped her learn the way
To call upon Manner-Man, help save the day,
Just say, "I am strong, and my flash is bright,
And I will defend you and make things all right."
So Elisabeth's now joined the Manner-Man Team,
Rescuing kids from the ones who are mean.

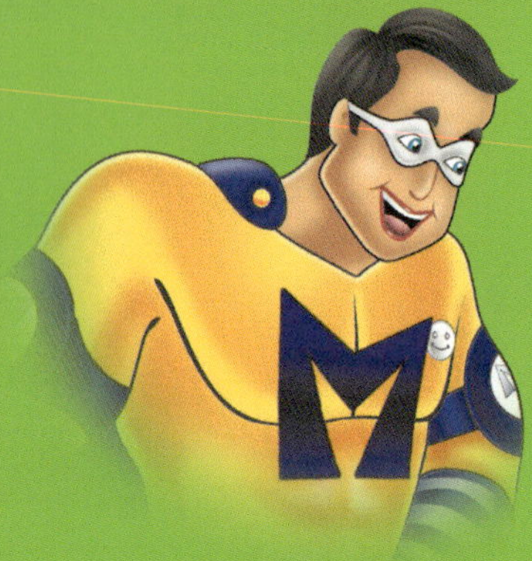

No matter the problem, no matter the crime,
Manner-Man saves the day, time after time.
He teaches good manners, so take his advice:
If someone starts shoving, just shout out "Not nice!"

So please think of others and treat them the way
You'd like to be treated at home and at play.
Be careful to not hurt with words that you say,
And try hard to do a good deed every day.

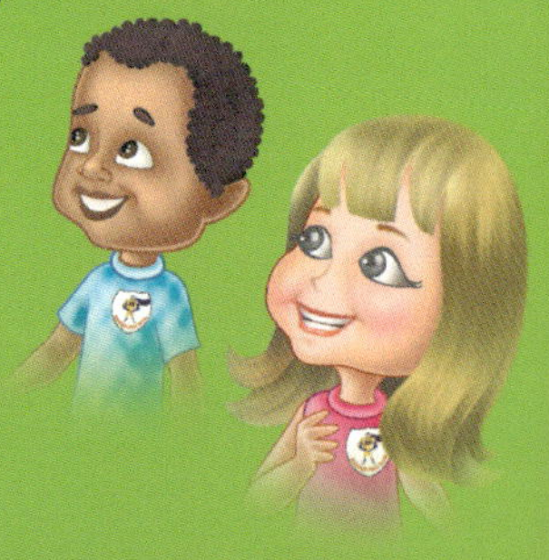

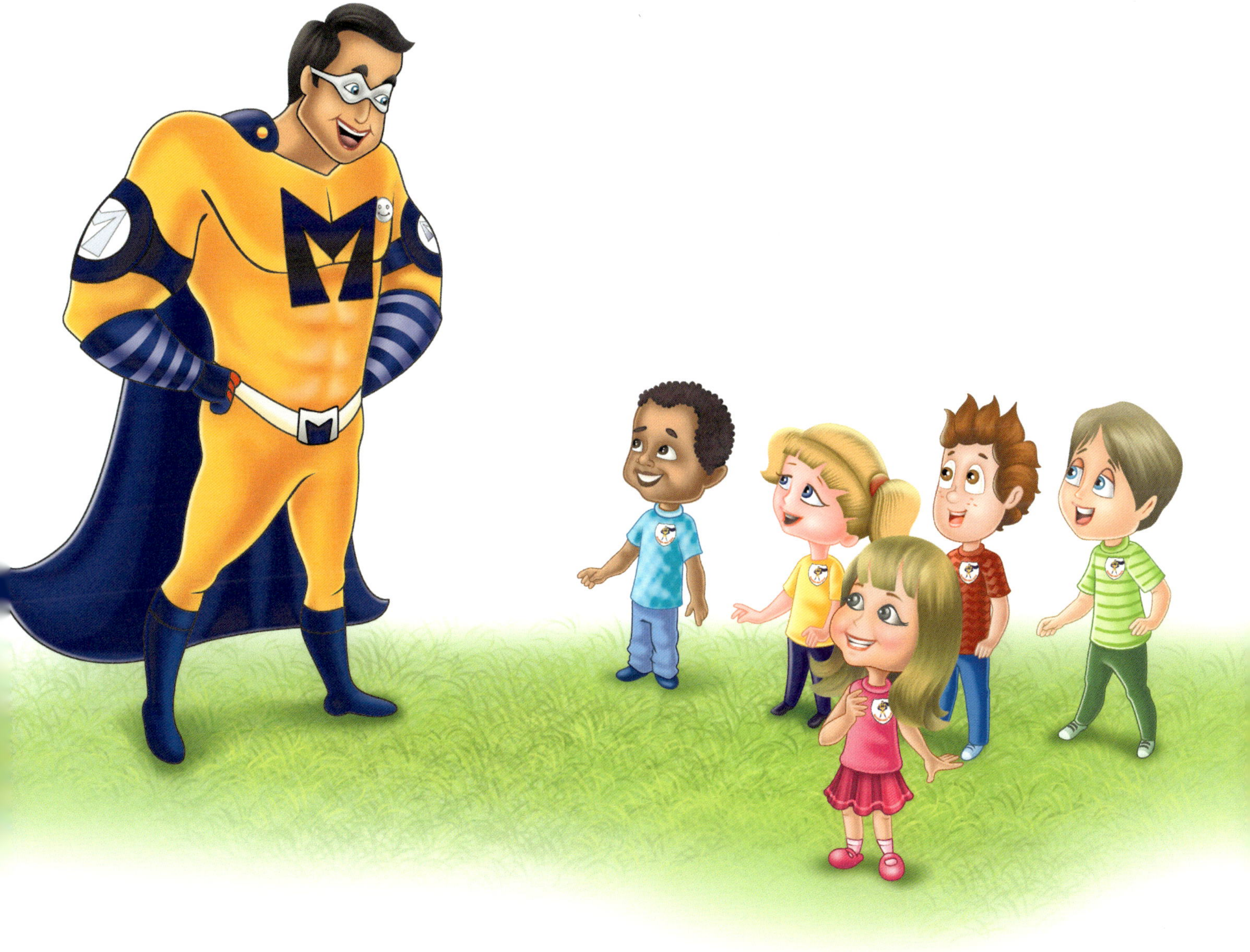

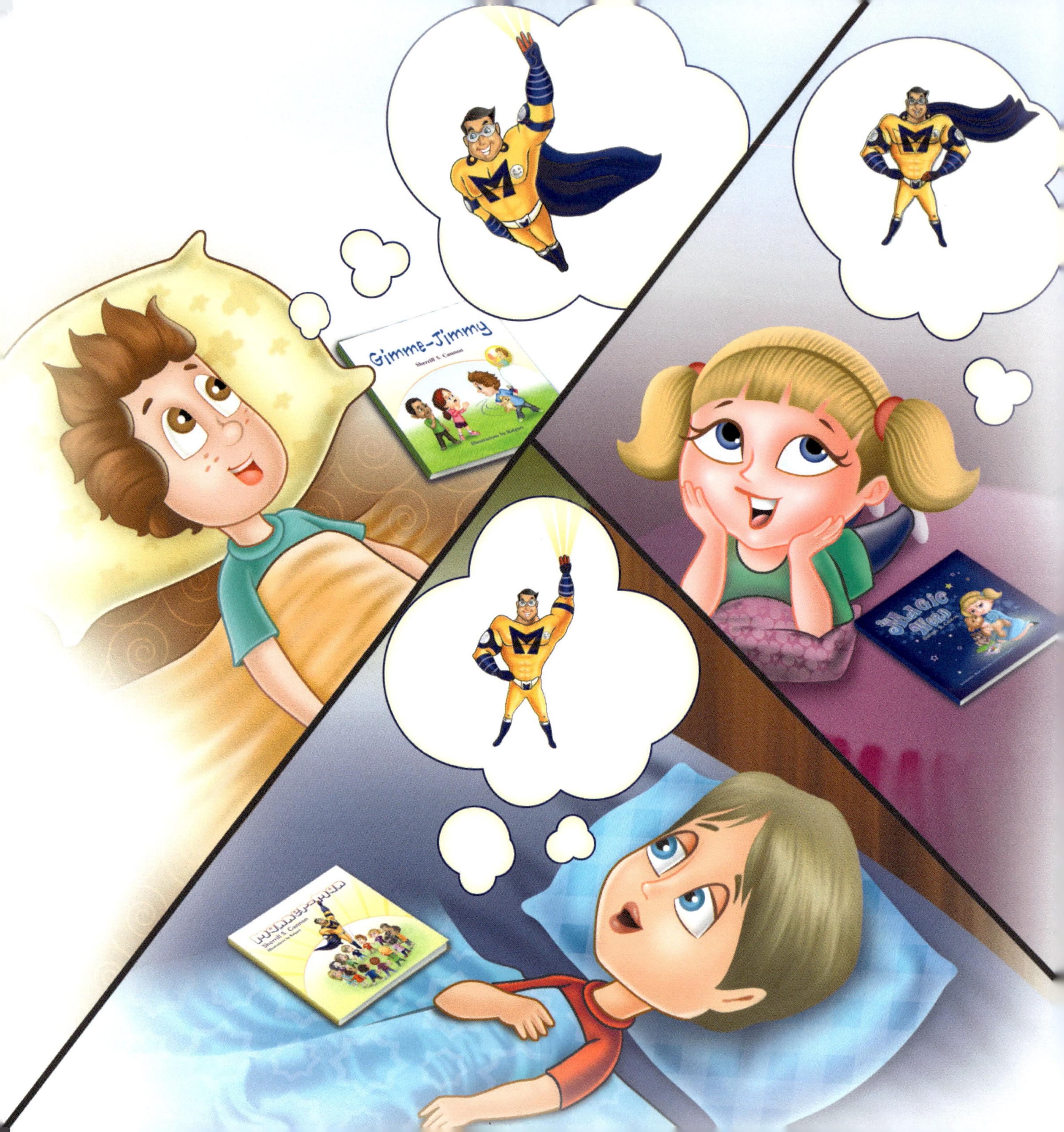
Gimme-Jimmy
Sherrill S. Cannon

James and Elisabeth now help our friends,
We call upon Manner-Man again and again.
We all work together to do what we can
To follow the rules of our great Manner-Man.

The Manner-Man Team's always looking for those
Who try to help others and share what he knows.
Would you like to join us, be part of our team?
When you go to sleep, dream the Manner-Man dream.
Just say, "I am strong, and my flash is bright,
And I will defend you and make things all right."
Then put on your badge, and wear it with pride—
And always remember your hero's inside . . .

Please consider these other award winning books by Sherrill S. Cannon:

Gimme-Jimmy
Sherrill S. Cannon

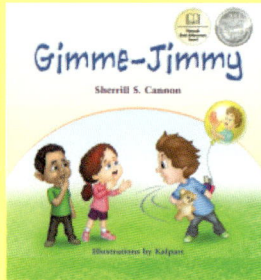

Winner of the 2012 Readers Favorite Silver Medal Award and the 2012 Pinnacle Achievement Winner Award

Gimme-Jimmy is about how a bully learns to share. His "New Polite Rule" helps him learn to make friends.

ISBN 978-1-61897-267-5

The Magic Word
Sherrill S. Cannon

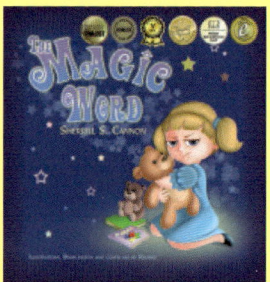

Winner of six awards: the 2011 Readers Favorite Gold Medal, 2011 Pinnacle Achievement Award Winner, 2011 Global Finalist Award, 2012 Reader Views Second Place, 2012 International Book Awards Finalist, and 2012 Next Generation Indie Finalist.

Elisabeth needs to learn *The Magic Word* "please", and to use it every day. Please and Thank you are words that everyone needs to use!

ISBN 978-1-6096-909-3

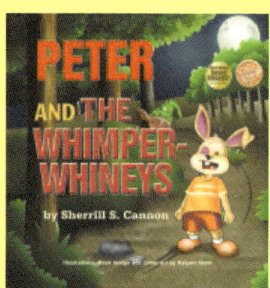

PETER
AND THE
WHIMPER-
WHINEYS
by Sherrill S. Cannon

Winner of the 2011 Readers Favorite Bronze Medal and the 2011 USA Best Books Finalist Award

Peter and the Whimper-Whineys helps parents cope with whining, disguised as a fun story. Peter is a rabbit who whines all the time, and might have to join the Whimper-Whineys.

ISBN 978-1-60911-517-3

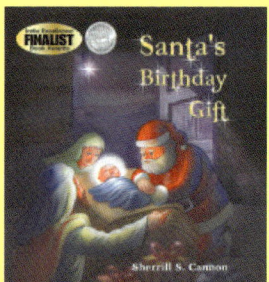

FINALIST
Santa's
Birthday
Gift
Sherrill S. Cannon

Winner of the 2011 Readers Favorite Silver Award and the 2011 Indie Excellence Finalist Award.

Santa's Birthday Gift includes Santa in the Christmas story.

(After reading a story of the nativity to my granddaughter, she asked "But where's Santa?")

ISBN 978-1-60860-824-9

All of Sherrill S. Cannon's books are available at http://sbpra.com/curejm where 50% of the cost of the books goes to the CureJM Foundation to help find a cure for Juvenile Myositis, an incurable children's disease. Let's find a cure!

Acknowledgements

A very special Thank You to KJ and her team of artists at Kalpart who again have brought to life one of my books, and made me proud to have people judge my books by their covers – for the fifth time!!

Thank you again to my publisher SBPRA - especially Robert, Lynn and Kait

And also to Ellen, Georgie, Denise, Suzann, Felicia, Kim, Lee, Liz, Amanda and Darya

Congratulations to my special kids who are already part of the Manner-Man team:

Captain: Addie - Team Members: Annalise, Anthony, Brenna, Danielle, Dominic, Greysen, Hannah, Isabel, Joey, Johnathon, Joseph, Katelynn, Kathryn, Landon, Logan, Maggie, Mason, Mckenna, Paige, Savannah, Shane, Tessa, Vinny, Wilkie –
Angels: Allison, Ana, Avielle, Benjamin, Caroline, Catherine, Charlotte, Chase, Daniel, Dylan, Emilie, Grace, Jack, James, Jesse, Jessica, Josephine, Madeleine, Noah, Olivia

With gratitude to those who have helped me share my books with others:

Shari, Tertia, Julian, Kate, Rebecca, Pat, Gail, Jon, Verna, Yvonne and Jannifer

Thanks to my family – you know who you are!

Note to my readers

Can you find my other covers in this book?
(*Peter and the Whimper-Whineys, The Magic Word, and Gimme-Jimmy.*)

Do you recognize any of the children from my other books in the scenes?

Can you find Addie from the CureJM Foundation website?
(http://sbpra.com/cureJM/)

Can you find the red M on Manner-Man?
(Look for the Red M on his left hand fingers!)

Would you like a Manner-Man Badge Sticker?
Please contact me at my website:
http://www.sherrillcannon.com

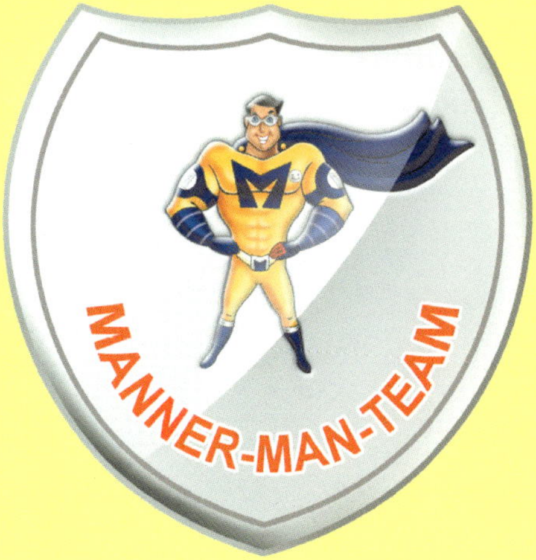
MANNER-MAN-TEAM

Manner-Man Badge

(Cut Out)

CPSIA information can be obtained
at www.ICGtesting.com
Printed in the USA
BVIC01n0853221013
334314BV00001B